THE PATCHWORK CAT

Nicola Bayley
& William Mayne

PUFFIN BOOKS

For Sheila, Doreen and Margaret   W.M.

For John Hilton   N.B.

"Good morning, good yawning,"
says Tabby, getting up. She
stretches.

She sleeps on a quilt. It is patchwork, like herself. She loves it.

She loves her breakfast too. She waits for it.

She says good morning, and good yawning to the people who live in her house.

They are a mother and a father and two children.

They all watch for the milkman. Tabby's tail begins to twitch.

They hear his float, they hear him sing.

Tabby goes out and loves the milkman.

"Oh milkman, milkman," she says, "you can come and live at my house any time."

Milk is poured for her.

After breakfast Tabby goes to have another little rest.

But she cannot find the patchwork quilt, her matching, patchwork quilt.

"Ah," says the mother, "we have done some snatchwork on your patchwork. We have thrown it out because it is so very dirty, and we shall buy a basket."

Tabby does not want a basket. She will do some angry scratchwork on it if it comes.

"I think I should send this family away," she says. "I shall have the milkman here to lodge instead."

She goes to look for her
patchwork quilt, to wash herself
and stretch and sleep.

She finds it. It is in the rubbish
bin. She reaches up and touches it.
She climbs in under the lid with it,
and goes to sleep.

Then bang and crash, and black
and thick the dark.

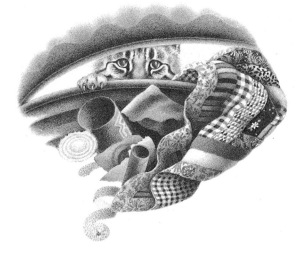

The lid is tightly on, the bin is in the air and upside-down. Tabby falls out, wrapped in her patchwork quilt.

She is in the rubbish truck. She sits and cries with no one there to hear. The engines and the shaking and the dangers and the quaking catch her calls.

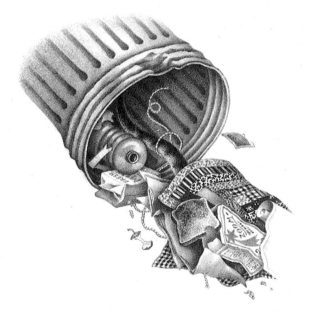

She is going on a journey. She is scared. She does not like it much.

She hisses and she arches up her back, but no one knows.

The journey ends. The truck lifts up its back and hisses. It tips out Tabby and her patchwork quilt.

Where she is she cannot tell.
There is nothing good to see and
nothing good to smell.

She does not like to touch. She
sees that all this place is rubbish.
She has to dodge aside, here comes
another batch.

And then another, until the day
is over. The last truck goes; the
driver latches up the gate.

Tabby is in the dump and cannot get out.

She says, "I am a sorry wretch."

Darkness comes. Rats wake up and gnash their teeth at her and flash their eyes.

They watch and make her rage with fright. She guards her patchwork quilt all night, and growls and squalls.

At morning time the rats go home. The gates are opened once again. The trucks begin to pitch the rubbish in.

Tabby drags her patchwork quilt up to the gate. She will not let it go.

She waits until a truck has left, and with her quilt she follows up the track.

She hopes a truck will not come by and crush the patchwork quilt or crunch her bones. She crawls along the ditch.

She holds a corner of the patchwork in her mouth, and has to clench her teeth.

She comes safely out. But she is far from home and does not know how long she'll have to trudge.

She will not go without the patchwork quilt.

Her teeth begin to ache.

She goes along a street and does not know the way. Each turning might be wrong. Which one to take she cannot tell.

She hopes she does not meet a cruel dog or bitch.

Then she hears a sound she knows, and the voice she loves the best. Her tail begins to twitch.

The milkman in his float is there,
the rich voice sings a morning song.
"Good morning," says the
milkman, "here's Tabby far from
home and lost. Come up with me,
and I'll soon fetch you to your
kitchen, with your pretty patchwork quilt that's all the fashion."

Tabby sits beside him on her patchwork quilt, and licks herself.

The milkman pours fresh milk to drink. Tabby is hitch-hiking home.

At home the mother and the father and the children are very pleased to see that she is found.

Tabby thinks that they can stay,
if the milkman will promise to
come each day.

The mother says that she must
wash the patchwork quilt to make it
fresh, and mend it with a stitch or
two to make it new.

Tabby says, "I'll be tired soon,
so wash it now."

When it's clean she sleeps till
dinner time, then wakes and says,
"Good morning, good yawning,"
and has a great big stretch.

She makes sure she is home, and
goes to sleep again all afternoon.

Contents

What is a truck? 4

Parts of a truck 6

Lots of wheels 8

Inside the cab 10

A powerful engine 12

Carrying goods 14

Transporting animals 16

Carrying cars 18

Tankers 20

Off-road trucks 22

Small trucks 24

The biggest trucks 26

Special trucks 28

Truck activities 30

Glossary and Further information 31

Index 32

What is a truck?

Trucks are huge vehicles with big, powerful engines. You have probably seen them on roads, towering over all the cars.

Trucks are used to pull **loads** that are too heavy or too big to be taken by car. They are all designed to carry different loads.

The load might be anything. It could be televisions, crisps, milk, animals or a great big digger!

Truck fact!

Some trucks can even carry houses! The frame of the house is made in one place and then a truck carries it to another place.

Parts of a truck

Look at all the parts of a truck!

Trucks have two main parts, the **tractor** and the **trailer**. Sometimes the tractor and trailer are permanently fixed together. These are called 'straight' or '**rigid**' trucks.

This is a rigid truck.

Tractor
The front part of the truck, with the cab and the engine.

Cab
The driver sits in the cab.

Trailer
This carries the **load**.

Engine
Truck **engines** are big and powerful.

Some tractors can fix on to different types of trailer. When a tractor and trailer are joined together, it is called an '**articulated**' truck.

This is an articulated truck.

Trailer

Tractor

Wheels

Lights
Trucks need lots of lights so that other drivers can see them.

Truck fact!
Truck brakes work using air. That is why you hear a 'pssshhhtt' sound when a truck brakes!

Lots of wheels

Trucks are built on a strong frame called a **chassis**. **Axles** are attached to the chassis. The wheels are attached to each end of the axles.

Chassis

Dual wheels

Trucks often have **dual wheels**. This means two wheels are attached side-by-side to each end of the axle.

Truck fact!

The biggest lorries are known as '18-wheelers'. They have 18 wheels altogether.

Some trucks pull light loads, so they only need two sets of wheels. They have one set of wheels under the tractor and one set under the trailer.

Bigger trucks pull much heavier loads, so they need more wheels. Some trucks have as many as eight sets of wheels.

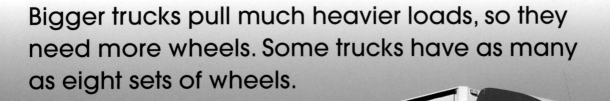

Inside the cab

The truck driver sits in the cab. Truck controls are similar to those in a car. There is a steering wheel, a hand brake and levers for the lights, **indicators** and windscreen wipers.

Steering wheel

Truck drivers need good **visibility**. This means they can see clearly all around. Big windows and mirrors are important. Mirrors help truck drivers to see what is happening at the sides of the truck and behind it.

As trucks travel long distances, most of them have a rest area behind the driver's seat. There is space for a bed, and in big cabs there is space for a fridge and television as well.

Truck fact!

Some truck drivers travel such a long way that they can be away from home for several days.

A powerful engine

The engine is the most important part of the truck. In some trucks, the engine is under the bonnet in front of the cab. The bonnet lifts up if someone needs to look at the engine.

Engine

Bonnet

In other trucks, the engine is under the cab. The cab tilts forward if the engine needs to be fixed.

Truck engines need a lot of fuel. Most of them run on **diesel**. The diesel is pumped into the engine from the fuel tank.

Fuel tank

Truck fact!
Some trucks have a fuel tank that can carry up to 1,500 litres! The average car fuel tank holds about 60 litres.

Carrying goods

Trucks are used to carry 'goods'. Goods can be anything, from freezers to food to bicycles!

Goods trucks look like big boxes. Some have a door at the back that is opened to load or unload the trailer. Others can be loaded from the side.

The sides of the truck are made from tough material and are tied shut. These are called curtain-sided trucks.

Truck fact!

Many trucks are 13 metres long. That's the same as 12 seven-year-olds lying head to toe.

Goods can be transported in big metal boxes called containers. These are carried by container trucks. Container trucks have **flatbed trailers**. Containers (below) are lifted onto the trailer and fixed in place.

Trucks with flatbed trailers are also used to transport more unusual loads, such as large tanks or big machines.

Transporting animals

Animals are **transported** in a special truck. The truck must be safe so that the animals are not injured on the journey.

Big **livestock** trucks transport sheep and pigs. Some trucks have many layers, so the animals have to walk up a ramp to get in. There are holes in the sides of the truck to let air in.

Bigger animals, such as horses, can also be transported in trucks. Horse transporters have separate spaces for each horse and hay baskets so that horses can eat while they are going along.

Truck fact!
The biggest livestock trucks have three layers. They can carry over 700 lambs.

Carrying cars

Cars can also be transported on trucks.
You might have seen huge car transporters
when you have been travelling on big roads.

Car transport trucks have two layers that can
move. To load the cars onto the truck, the top
layer is lowered to the ground and the cars
are driven on. Then it is lifted up again. The
same happens with the lower layer.

Truck fact!

Most car transporters can carry up to ten cars. Some carry ordinary road cars, while others transport racing cars.

Breakdown trucks also carry cars. They collect cars that have broken down and take them back to the garage to be mended.

Tankers

Trucks that carry liquids are called **tankers**. A tanker has a big container on the back. They can carry liquids, such as oil and milk.

Tankers are loaded through a pipe. The pipe squirts liquid into the tank. When it is full the tank is **sealed**.

Truck fact!
Some tankers can carry up to 35,000 litres. That's 100,000 cans of drink!

A cement mixer is a special type of tanker. Cement needs to be kept moving so that it doesn't set, or go hard. The **drum** of the cement mixer keeps turning while it drives along, so that the cement stays runny.

Drum

Off-road trucks

Trucks are designed to work off the roads too. They can travel over rough ground or slippery ice.

Some trucks are made to carry **timber**. They collect cut timber from the forest and take it to the saw mill. Timber trucks must be able to travel on muddy forest roads.

Truck fact!

Some of the biggest timber trucks can carry up to 45 tonnes of timber.

Tipper trucks are used at construction sites and quarries. They have a big open trailer that can be filled with rocks and earth.

When it is time to empty the trailer, the front end lifts up in the air and the contents are tipped out.

23

Small trucks

Small trucks carry small loads. A delivery truck takes goods to individual people. It collects the goods from the **depot** in the morning and takes them to lots of people in different places during the day. When the truck is empty, it goes back to the depot.

Some people have pick-up trucks at home.
These are like cars, but they have a big open
back instead of a boot. This is called the **bed**.

Bed

Pick-up trucks are used to carry tools or to move
things around. Although they are small, they
can be very powerful.

Truck fact!
There are some small trucks that run on electric power.

The biggest trucks

The biggest trucks are very powerful. The tractors are built to pull vast loads over long distances.

In some countries where trucks need to pull loads a long distance, some companies use road trains.

These are trucks that pull more than one trailer. Some pull two and others pull lots more.

Truck fact!

The world record for the longest road train was set in Australia. The road train was pulling 112 trailers!

The biggest off-road trucks are used in mining.
Their wheels are bigger than any adult.

Some mining trucks can be over 15 metres long
and eight metres high!

Special trucks

Not all trucks are made for carrying loads.
Some are built for sport. They are used in
rallying and racing. Some are built to be
the fastest or the toughest.

Some trucks compete in races, such as the
Dakar Rally. This is a race that takes many
days and goes through the Sahara desert.

Jet-engine trucks are fitted with the same engines as jet planes. They are built to travel very fast.

Monster trucks are made to perform stunts. They jump over long lines of cars and race each other in front of excited crowds.

Truck fact!

Jet-engine trucks can travel at over 480 kilometres an hour!

Truck activities

History: How do you think goods and animals were transported before big trucks were invented?

Geography: Which countries do you think use the biggest trucks and why?

Art: Design a truck to carry a special load. What makes your truck different from others?

Literacy: Write a story about a truck journey that takes many days. What do you think it would be like to sleep in the cab?

Design & Technology: Make a model of a truck. Think about what kind of materials you need to make it strong.

Glossary

articulated a truck with a tractor and trailer that are joined together but can be taken apart

axles strong bars that are fixed across the chassis; the wheels are attached to these

bed the big open area at the back of a pick-up truck

chassis the frame on which a truck is built

depot a warehouse where goods are stored

diesel a type of liquid fuel

drum the container on the back of a cement mixer that carries the cement

dual wheels two wheels fixed side by side on the end of an axle

flatbed trailer a trailer with a flat load area that can carry many different loads

indicators small coloured lights that signal which way a vehicle is going to turn

livestock animals kept on a farm, such as sheep, cows or pigs

load something that is carried

rigid a truck that has a tractor and trailer that are permanently joined together

sealed closed tightly

tanker a truck that carries liquid

timber trees that have been cut down

tractor the front part of the truck, with the engine and the cab

trailer the back part of the truck that carries the load

transport move from one place to another

visibility the ability to be seen or see things clearly

Further information

Mighty Trucks (Amazing Machines), Chris Oxlade, Franklin Watts, 2007.

This Is My Truck (Mega Machine Drivers), Chris Oxlade, Franklin Watts, 2006.

Trucks (Big Machines), David and Penny Glover, Franklin Watts, 2007.

Trucks (DK Machines at Work), Elizabeth Haldane, Dorling Kindersley, 2005.

Trucks (Machines Inside Out), Chris Oxlade, Wayland, 2008.

Trucks (On The Go), David and Penny Glover, Wayland, 2007.

Index

animals 16–17
articulated truck 7
axles 8

bonnet 12
brakes 7
breakdown truck 19

cab 6, 10–11,
cars 4, 10, 13, 18–19, 25
cement mixer 21
chassis 8
container trucks 15
curtain-sided trucks 14

delivery truck 24
driver 10

engines 4, 6, 12–13, 29

flatbed trailers 15
fuel 13

goods 14–15

horse transporter 17

jet-engine trucks 29

lights 7, 10
livestock trucks 16
loads 4, 5, 6, 9

mining trucks 27
mirrors 10
monster trucks 29

pick-up trucks 25

rest area 11
rigid trucks 6
road trains 26

tankers 20–21
timber trucks 22
tipper trucks 23
tractor 6, 7, 9, 26
trailers 6, 7, 9, 14, 15, 23, 26

wheels 6, 8–9, 27

YPS
M

This Walker book belongs to:

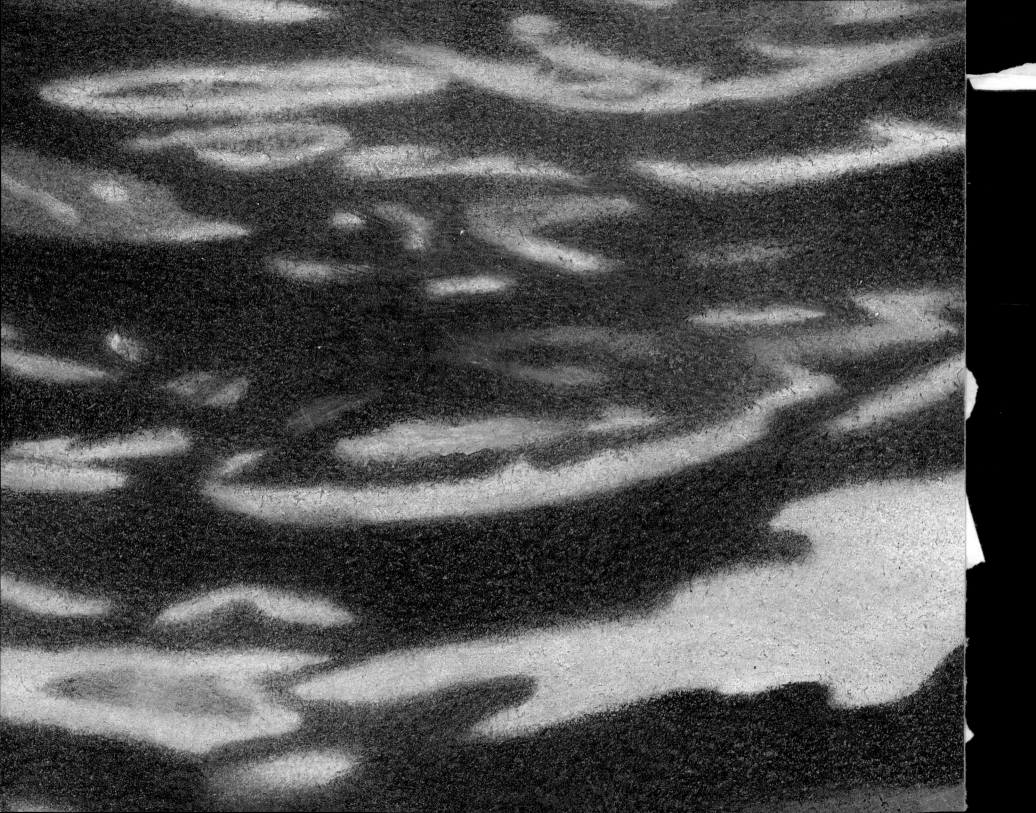

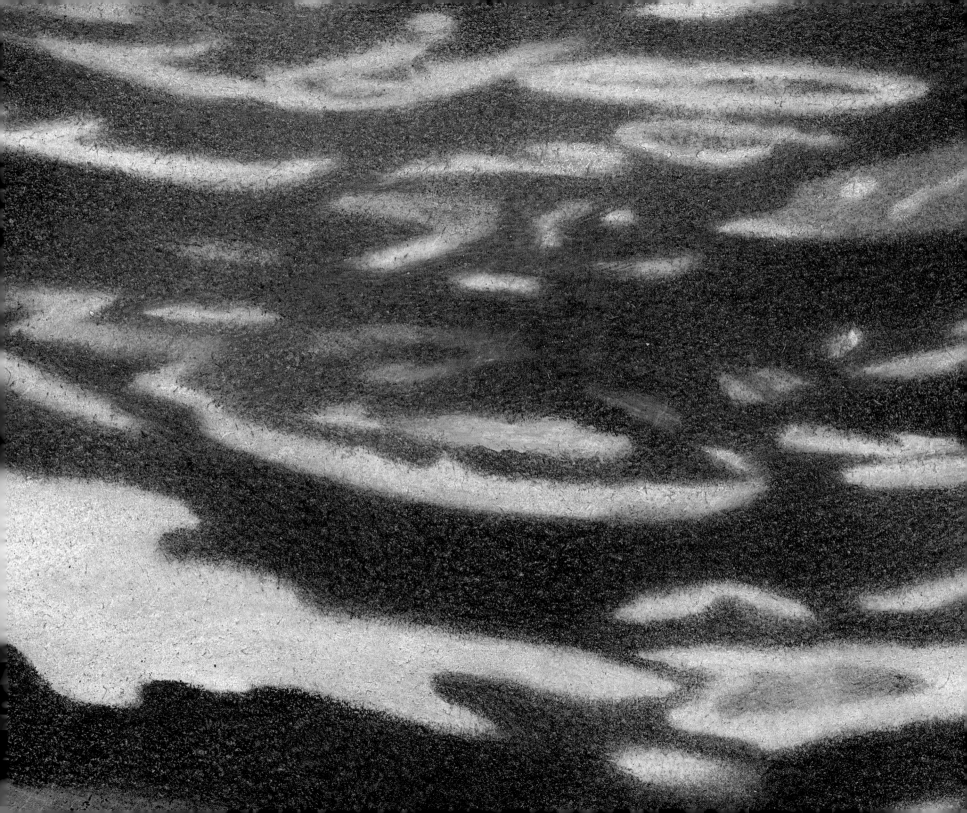

For D.L.
M.W.

For W.A.D.
J.E.

First published 1994 by Walker Books Ltd
87 Vauxhall Walk, London SE11 5HJ

This edition published 2009

4 6 8 10 9 7 5

Text © 1994 Martin Waddell
Illustrations © 1994 Jennifer Eachus

The right of Martin Waddell and Jennifer Eachus to be identified as author and illustrator respectively of this work
has been asserted by them in accordance with the Copyright, Designs and Patents Act 1988

This book has been typeset in Bauer Bodoni

Printed in China

British Library Cataloguing in Publication Data:
a catalogue record for this book is available from the British Library

ISBN 978-1-4063-2324-5

www.walker.co.uk

The Big Big Sea

MARTIN WADDELL

Illustrated by
JENNIFER EACHUS

WALKER BOOKS
AND SUBSIDIARIES
LONDON · BOSTON · SYDNEY · AUCKLAND

Mum said, "Let's go!"
So we went…

out of the house
and into the dark
and I saw…
THE MOON.

We went over the field
and under the fence
and I saw
the sea in the moonlight,
waiting for me.

And I ran
and Mum ran.
We ran and we ran
straight through the puddles
and out to the sea!

I went right in
to the shiny bit.
There was only me
in the big big sea.

I splashed
and I laughed
and Mum came after me
and we paddled
out deep in the water.

We got all wet.

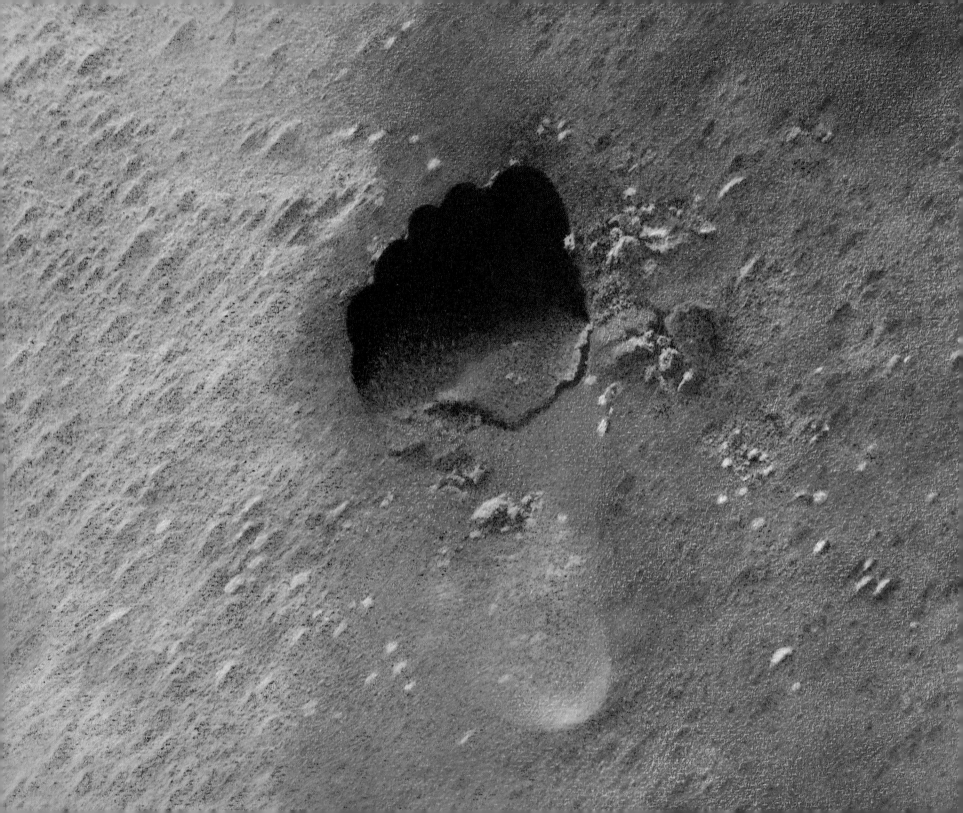

Then we walked
a bit more
by the edge of the sea
and our feet
made big holes
in the sand.

Far far away
right round the bay
were the town
and the lights
and the mountains.
We felt very small,
Mum and me.

We didn't go to the town.
We just stayed for a while
by the sea.

And Mum said to me,
"Remember this time.
It's the way life should be."

I got cold
and Mum carried me
all the way back.

We sat by the fire,
Mum and me,
and ate hot buttered toast
and I went to sleep
on her knee.

I'll always remember
just Mum and me
and the night
that we walked
by the big big sea.

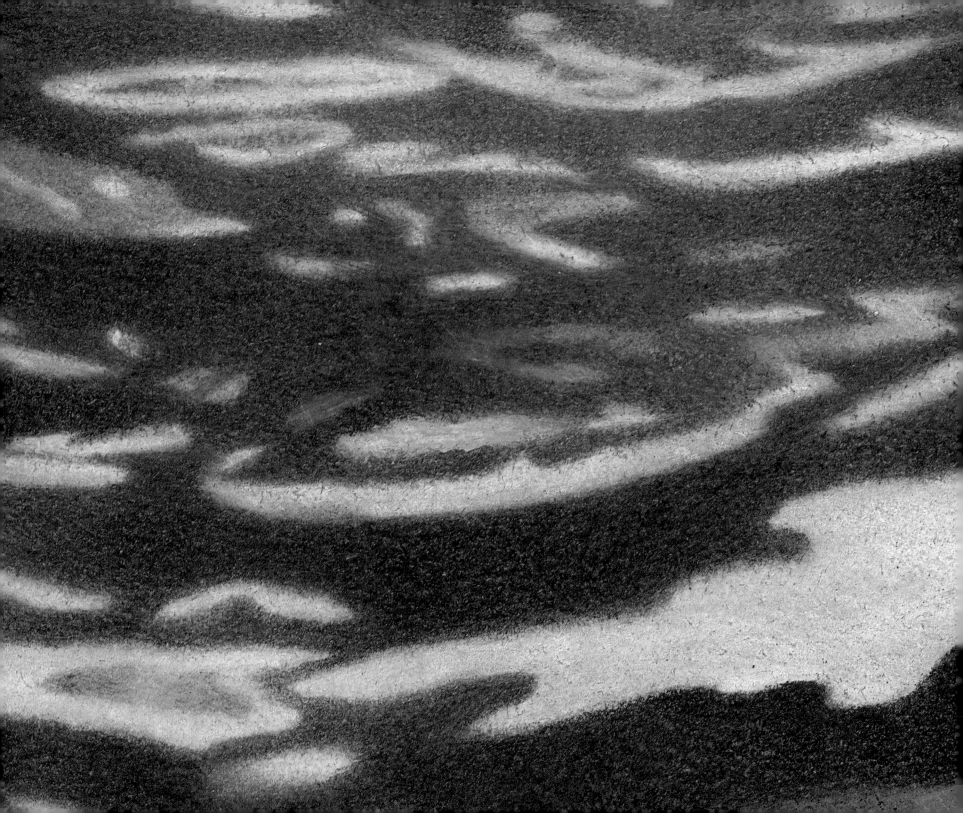

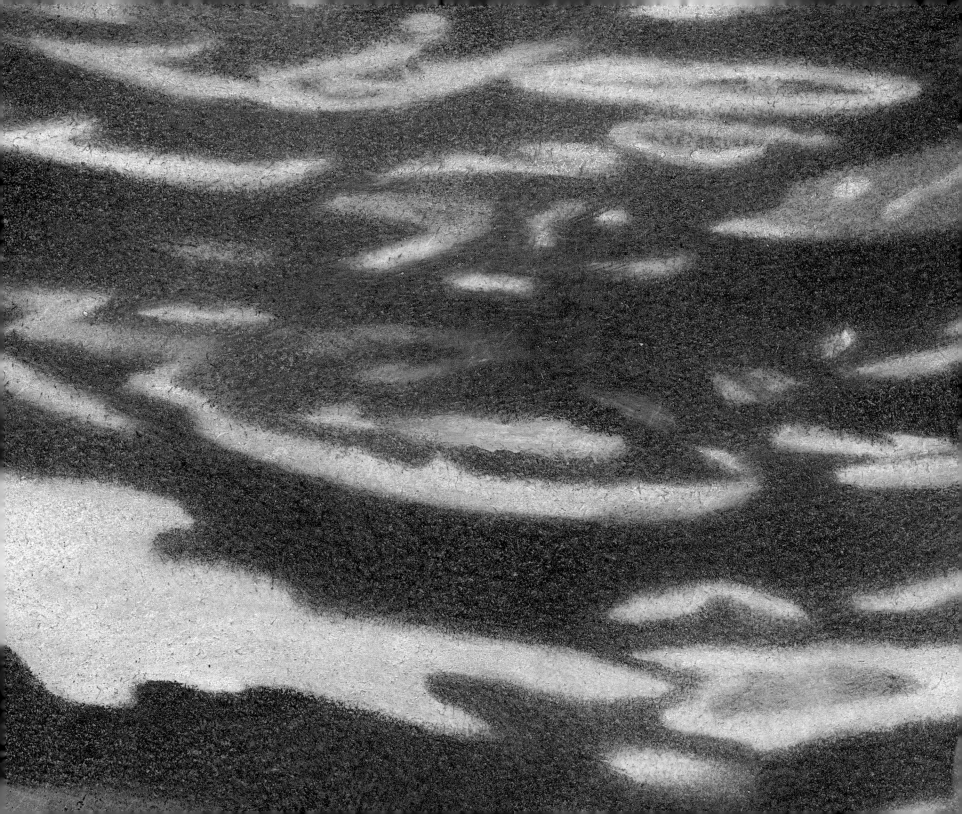

Other classic picture books from Martin Waddell

ISBN 978-1-84428-491-7

ISBN 978-1-84428-492-4

ISBN 978-1-84428-494-8

ISBN 978-1-84428-493-1

ISBN 978-0-7445-4067-3

ISBN 978-0-7445-3660-7

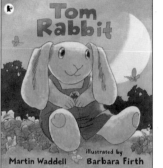

ISBN 978-0-7445-8280-2

ISBN 978-1-84428-538-9

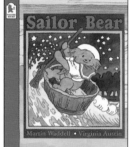

ISBN 978-0-7445-3150-3

ISBN 978-0-7445-9861-2

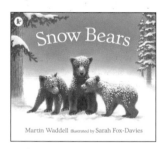

ISBN 978-0-7445-9892-6

ISBN 978-0-7445-3167-1

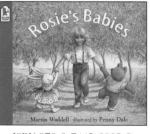

ISBN 978-0-7445-2335-5

ISBN 978-1-4063-0159-5

ISBN 978-1-4063-0098-7

ISBN 978-1-4063-0863-1

Available from all good booksellers

www.walker.co.uk